A GOOD DEED CAN GROW

For Nils, with love

—J.B.

It all started with planting my own good deed,
hiding a book in the forest. It led me to you
and grew a friendship. This book is for you.
Love ya, Amanda.

—H.H.

ABOUT THIS BOOK
The illustrations for this book were done in digital illustration and mixed media. This book was edited by Christy Ottaviano and designe Tracy Shaw. The production was supervised by Nyamekye Waliyaya, and the production editor was Annie McDonnell. The text was set in Al Sans, and the display type was hand lettered by Margaret Kimball.

 • Christy Ottaviano Books • Hachette Book Group • 1290 Avenue of the Americas, New York 10104 • Visit us at LBYR.com • First Edition: February 2023 • Christy Ottaviano Books is an imprint of Little, Brown and Company. • The Ch Ottaviano Books name and logo are trademarks of Hachette Book Group, Inc. • The publisher is not responsible for websites (or their con that are not owned by the publisher. • Library of Congress Cataloging-in-Publication Data • Names: Bertman, Jennifer Chambliss, aut Hatam, Holly, illustrator. • Title: A good deed can grow / by Jennifer Bertman ; illustrated by Holly Hatam. • Description: First edition. | York : Little, Brown and Company, 2023. | "Christy Ottaviano Books." | Audience: Ages 4–8. | Summary: "A gentle and lyrical picture book celebrates the importance and impact of good deeds, all by showcasing the magic of nature, kindness, and nurturing community"— Provid publisher. • Identifiers: LCCN 2021053991 | ISBN 9780316351133 (hardcover) • Subjects: CYAC: Conduct of life—Fiction. | Kindness—Fic Helpfulness—Fiction. • Classification: LCC PZ7.1.B46485 Go 2023 | DDC [E]—dc23 • LC record available at https://lccn.loc.gov/2021053
ISBN 978-0-316-35113-3 • Printed in China • RRD • 10 9 8 7 6 5 4 3 2 1

A GOOD DEED CAN GROW

JENNIFER
CHAMBLISS
BERTMAN

illustrated by
HOLLY HATAM

Christy Ottaviano Books
LITTLE, BROWN AND COMPANY
New York Boston

Seeds

A good deed
can grow like a seed.

A seed that sprouts into a dandelion
and travels from yard to yard . . .

and field to field,
and town to town.

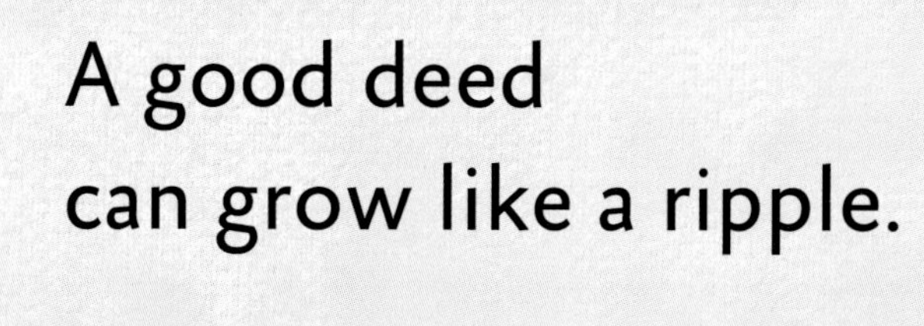

A good deed
can grow like a ripple.

A ripple that begins with a drop
and spreads into a circle . . .

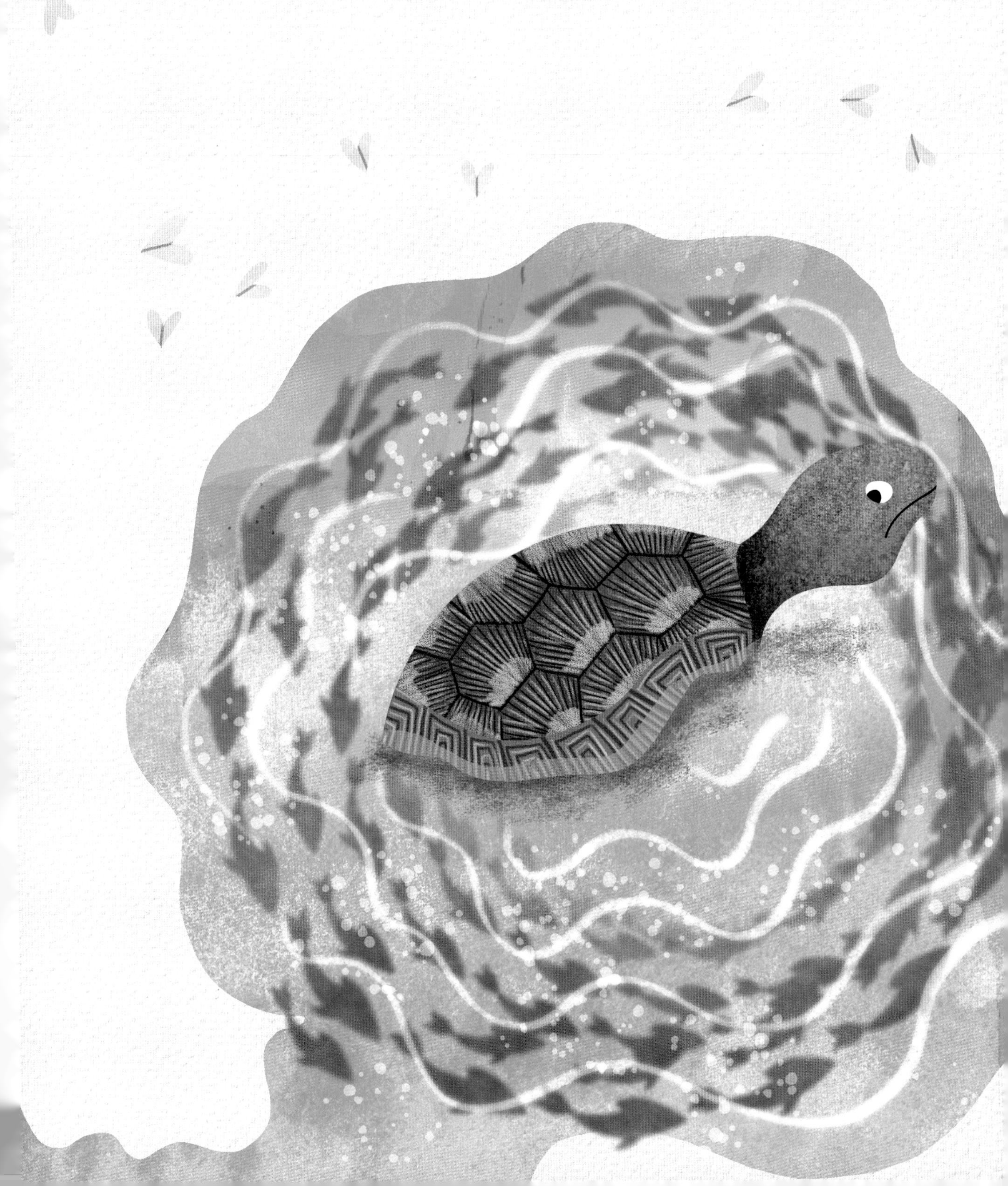

and ring after ring,
across an entire lake.

LEMONADE
Free Lemonade
Smile!
HAVE A GREAT DAY!

A good deed
can grow like a sunbeam.

A sunbeam that shines
through the clouds . . .

and transforms the dull to light,
the gray to bright.

A good deed
can grow like a smile.

SENIOR CENTER

A smile that calms worries and nerves,
warms hearts . . .

or welcomes you home.

Sometimes we might feel too small
to help a problem that seems so big.

Community Garden

When that happens,
remember all the goodness and
all the kindness that exist in our world
began somewhere, sometime ago . . .

as a seed,
a ripple,
a sunbeam,
a smile.

What good will you
grow today?